I0580353

Thinking Theory
BOOK FOUR
Created by Nicola Cantan

www.colourfulkeys.ie

What is Thinking Theory?

➡ Thinking Theory is a series of music theory workbooks designed to accelerate learning while providing plenty of reinforcement of each concept.

➡ Thinking Theory is designed so you can start anywhere in the series. Concepts are not left out of later books, just covered more quickly.

Concepts covered in this book...

➡ Note values: sixteenth note, eighth note, dotted eighth note, eighth note triplet, quarter note, dotted quarter note, half note, dotted half note & whole note

➡ Rest values: sixteenth note, eighth note, quarter note, half note & whole note

➡ Time signatures: 2/4 3/4 4/4 2/2 3/2 4/2 3/8 6/8 9/8 12/8 6/4 ¢ C

➡ Landmark notes: Low C, Bass C, Bass F, Middle C, Treble G, Treble C & High C

➡ Note stem rules

➡ Grouping sixteenth notes, eighth notes & rests

➡ Dynamics: Pianissimo, Piano, Mezzo Piano, Mezzo Forte, Forte, Fortissimo, Crescendo, Decrescendo, Diminuendo, Sempre Forte, Sempre Piano & Forte Piano

➡ Tempo marks: Poco Ritenuto, Poco Ritardando, Poco Rallentando, Ritenuto, Ritardando, Rallentando, Accelerando, A Tempo, Con Moto, Meno Mosso, Più Mosso, Presto, Vivace, Allegro, Allegretto, Moderato, Alla Marcia, Andante, Larghetto, Largo, Lento & Adagio

➡ Expression marks: Giocoso, Maestoso, Espressivo, Dolce, Grazioso & Cantabile

➡ Markings/symbols: pedal, accidentals, staccato, slurs, repeat marks, fermata, accent, strong accent, tenuto, 1st and 2nd endings, 8va & 8vb

➡ Solfa: Low Sol, Low La, Low Ti, Do, Re, Mi, Fa, Sol, La & High Do

➡ Scales: A minor, E minor, D minor, C major, G major, D major, F major & B♭ major

➡ Triads: A minor, E minor, D minor, C major, G major, D major, F major & B♭ major

➡ Intervals in the major scale

➡ Whole steps, half steps & enharmonics

Contents

About Nicola Cantan

Nicola Cantan began teaching piano in 2004, and has always strived to find new ways to engage students in learning. She uses games, improvisation and composing to accelerate her students' progress at the piano and broaden their musical knowledge.

Nicola wrote the 'Thinking Theory' books when she saw the struggle some of her students were having preparing for theory examinations. She wanted a book that regularly reinforced concepts in a systematic way, with a clean layout, and clear explanations . Thus 'Thinking Theory' was born.

FLASHCARD GAMES

All the flashcard games can be played with the corresponding Thinking Theory Flashcards which can be downloaded at www.colourfulkeys.ie/thinking-theory.

To play these games, the cards will need to printed one-sided, with the answer on a separate card. You may want to print two sets, one to be used as regular flashcards (printed back to back) and one to be used for games (printed on one side).

You can play these games with the flashcards for one or more chapters at a time, or with the complete set for the whole book. Games like these are a fantastic way to reinforce learning off the page, and allow drilling of concepts in a fun way. Try to revisit each flashcard set periodically by playing a different game, to foster long term and reliable memory.

MEMORY

1. This is a game for one or more players.
2. Lay out all the cards face down.
3. Turn over two cards at a time. If they match, put those cards aside. If they don't match, turn them back over.
4. Keep going until all cards have been matched.
5. (This game can also be played with multiple players taking turns.)

MATCH

1. This is a game for one player.
2. Lay out all the term cards face up on the floor.
3. See how fast you can match the answer cards by placing each card on top of the term that matches.
4. Time yourself and try to beat your time on the next go!

PAIRS

1. This is a game for two or more players.
2. Shuffle the cards and deal 4 to each player. Place the remainder of the cards in a pile between the players.
3. Each player takes turns to draw one card from the pile in the center.
4. If s/he has a matching pair, s/he should place it face up beside them.
5. The winner is the one with the most pairs when all the cards have been drawn.

SNAP

1. This is a game for two players.

2. Shuffle the cards and divide into two equal piles, one for each player.

3. On the count of three both players turn over the top card from her/his pile.

4. If the cards match, either player can shout "SNAP!".

5. The first player to say "SNAP!" wins all of the turned over cards, and adds them to her/his pile.

6. The winner is the first to win all the other cards or the one with the most cards when time is up.

GO FISH!

1. This is a game for two or more players.

2. Shuffle the cards and deal 5 to each player. Place the remainder of the cards in a pile between the players.

3. Each player takes turns to ask another player for cards that would match one of her/his own. For example "Got any E's?" or "Got a crescendo?".

4. The player can continue asking for more cards until the other player does not have the card they need and tells them to "Go fish!".

5. If told to "Go fish!" the player should pick up a card from the center pile.

6. As pairs are found, they should be placed face down in front of them.

7. The winner is the first to get rid of all her/his cards. If two players do this at the same time, the winner is the one with the most pairs.

CUCKOO

1. This is a game for two or more players.

2. Remove one card from the deck and place it aside.

3. Shuffle the cards and deal all the cards between the players. It's OK if some players get more cards than others.

4. Each player should sort through the cards and put down any pairs s/he finds without letting the other players see her/his cards.

5. One player at a time offers her/his cards (face down) to the player to her/his left.

6. The player to the left takes one card from her/his hand.

7. If this makes a pair, the player to the left puts the pair down beside her/him.

8. Continue like this until all the pairs have been found. The player left with the "Cuckoo" (the one that matches the card you took out)

9. is the loser.

➜ The circle of fifths is a useful tool for scales, keys and chord relationships.

➜ It's a good idea to get comfortable at drawing a circle of fifths quickly so that you can use it for reference until you remember these patterns.

Practice drawing a 12 evenly-spaced lines for your circle of fifths "clock" by drawing a plus shape and then 2 lines between each of those lines. Trace the dotted lines and then draw 3 more clock shapes in the boxes below.

 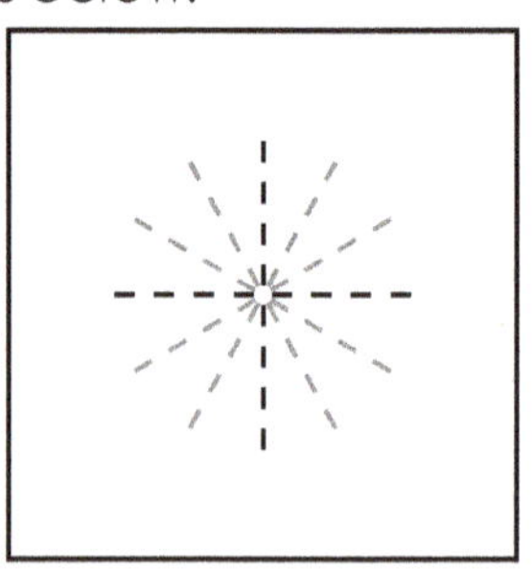  

Now add the letters. Start with a C at the top and then add the note a fifth higher going around clockwise until you reach B. Go back to C and add the note a fifth lower going around anti-clockwise. The first one has been partially done for you.

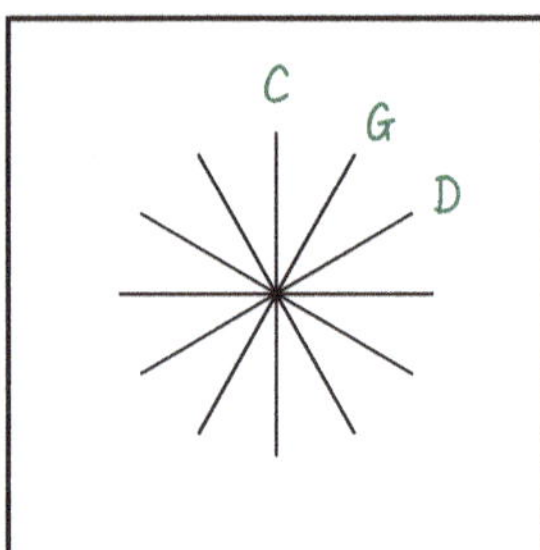   

Finally, add a flat beside the notes at 6 o'clock to 10 o'clock (to make these intervals perfect 5ths) and you will have drawn a complete major circle of fifths.

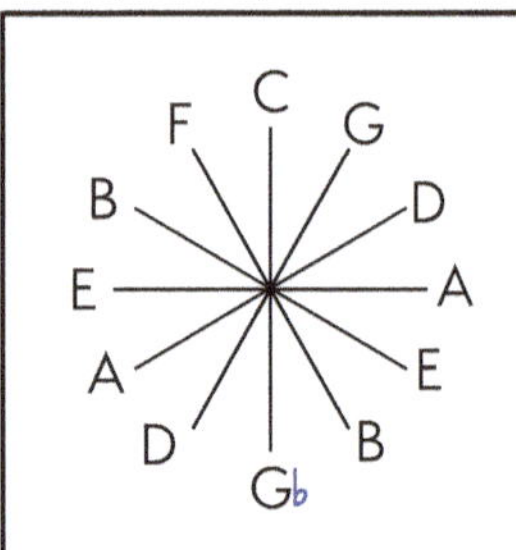   

Being able to draw a circle of fifths fast is extremely useful. Doodle them any chance you get!

Using the circle of fifths as a reference, write the major scale, ascending and descending, to match each of the key signatures below. (Start at C and count to the left for flats or to the right for sharps.)

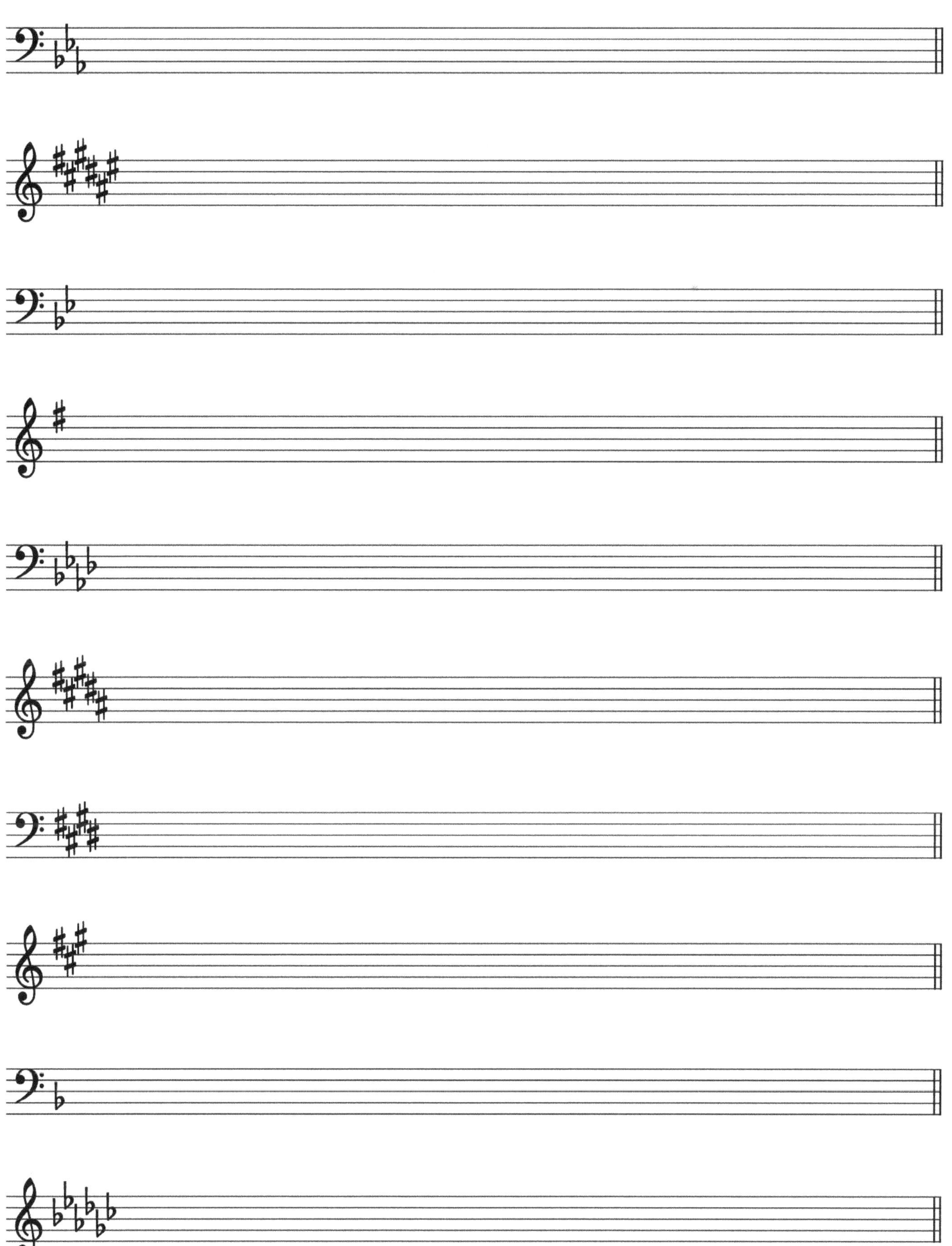

New Ingredients: Rhythm

♬ = sixteenth note = ¼ beat

♪ = eighth note = ½ beat

♩ = quarter note = 1 beat

𝅗𝅥 = half note = 2 beats

𝅗𝅥. = dotted half note = 3 beats

o = whole note = 4 beats

𝄾 = sixteenth rest = ¼ beat

𝄾 = eighth rest = ½ beat

𝄽 = quarter rest = 1 beat

▬ = half rest = 2 beats

▬ = whole rest = whole measure

³♫ = eighth note triplet = ⅓ beat each

✏ The glass on the left is labeled correctly. Circle the matching glass with the right amount of liquid.

  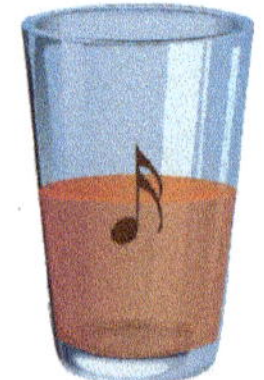  

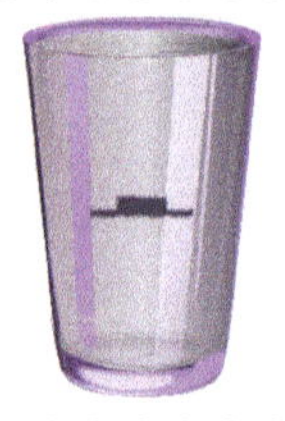    

    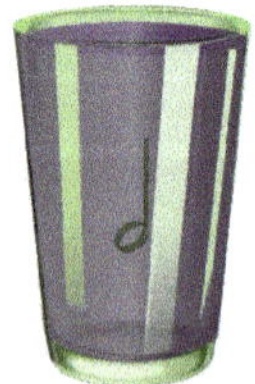

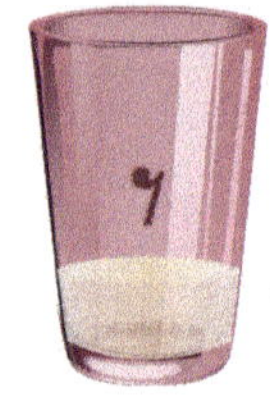    

- **Note Stem Rule 1:** If the note is line 3 or above, the stem goes down on the left of the notehead. If the note is space 2 or below, the stem goes up on the right of the notehead.
- **Note Stem Rule 2:** The stem should finish at the same note an octave above for upward stems, and at the same note an octave below for downward stems.
- **Note Stem Rule 3:** Stems of notes more than one ledger line away from the staff finish at the middle line.

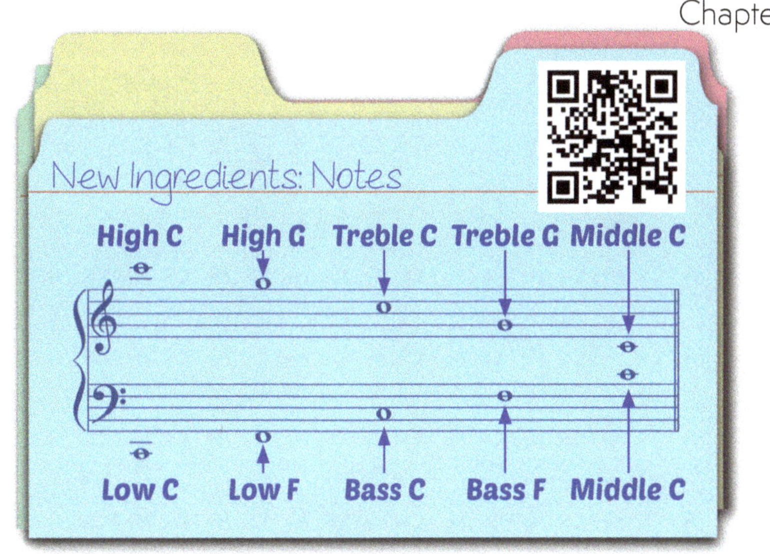

Write the name below each note & add stems to make the noteheads into quarter notes.

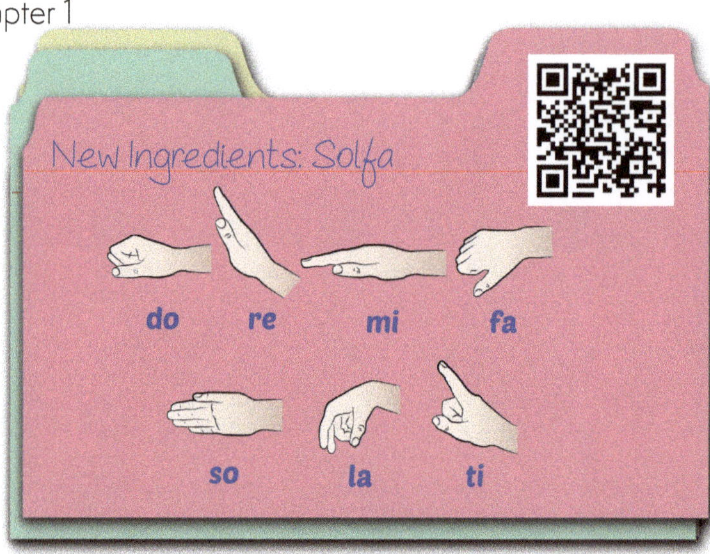

➡ Remember to use , for low notes and '
for high notes, e.g. *t*, for low ti and *d'* for
high do.

Sing the given melody 3 times.

Write the solfa initials under the notes and
then compose the missing measure.

Sing the full melody to check your work.

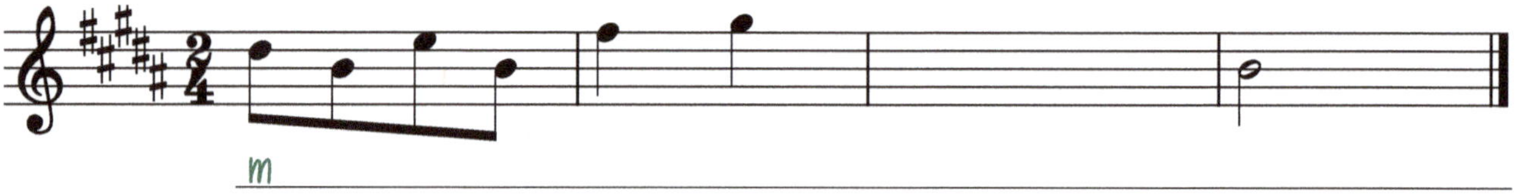

                © Copyright 2022 Vibrant Music Limited

✏ Match the Italian term or symbol on the left with its name or meaning on the right.

♪	decresc.	same sound written differently
		sixteenth note
⌢	rall.	quarter rest
		with a singing tone
poco rit.		gradually getting faster
allegretto		half note
	cantabile	fast
		slowly
○	a tempo	whole note
		portato
alla marcia	con moto	one half step lower
		sweetly
⁊		getting slower
	meno mosso	half rest
giocoso	più mosso	eighth rest
		more movement
▬	presto	loud then immediately soft
		gracefully
larghetto	vivace	quarter note
		accent
♩	♩♩♩	moderately quick
		one half step higher
whole step	moderato	two half steps
		walking pace
♩	espressivo	with movement
		always soft
♭		moderate speed
	⁊	lively
andante	sempre p	always loud
		emphasised
sempre f	dolce	marcato
		majestic
accelerando	maestoso	back to original speed
		gradually getting softer
fp	enharmonic	neighbouring notes
		fairly slowly
♩	♯	like a march
		getting a little slower
grazioso	half step	less movement
		fermata
lento	sf	eighth note triplet
		expressive
♫ (3)		playful/merry

Level Up!

Get ready for chapter 2 by answering these questions (without looking back through your book!)

1. Add note stems to these quarter note heads, then write in the note names underneath.

2. Draw a circle of fifths in each box.

3. Write the ascending major scale to match each of the key signatures below in eighth notes.

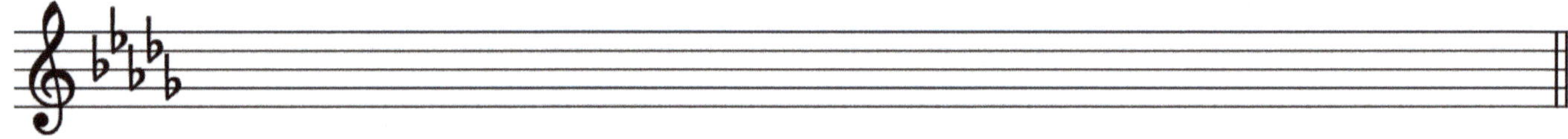

4. Write the descending major scale to match each of the key signatures below in half notes.

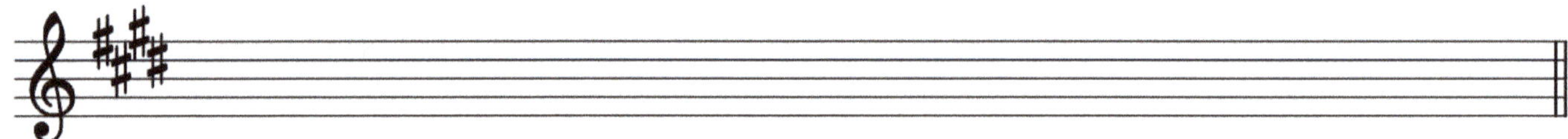

5. Write one note equal to the total value of each group.

- ➤ An interval is the distance between two notes.
- ➤ A harmonic interval is the distance between two notes which sound together.
- ➤ A melodic interval is the distance between two notes which sound one after the other.

Draw notes above the given notes to create harmonic intervals. Label each one as major or perfect.

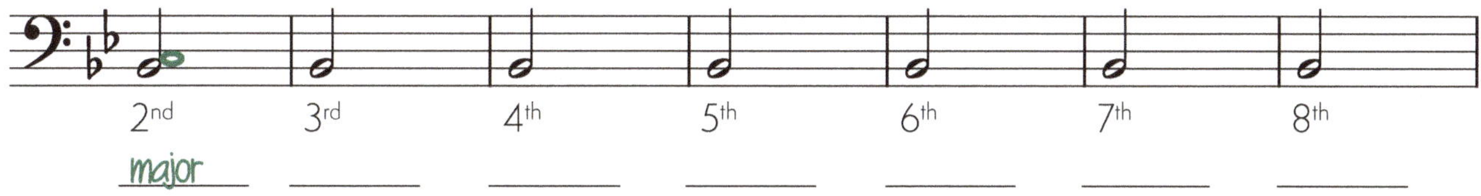

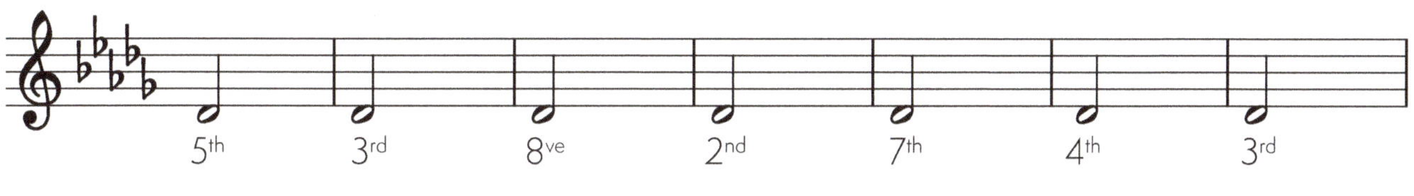

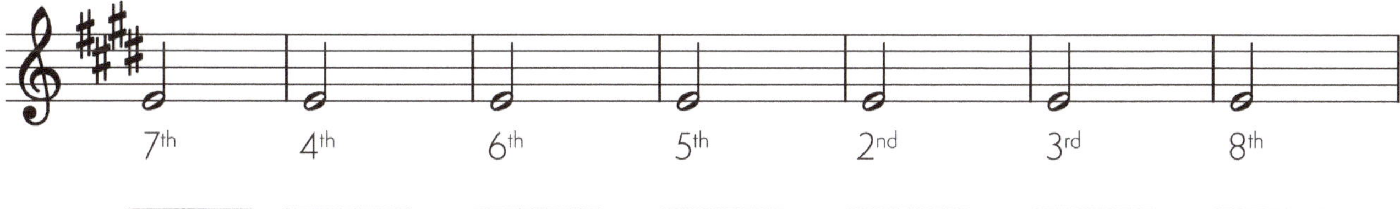

Label each of these melodic intervals with the interval number and quality.

✏ Draw a major circle of fifths in each circle below. Go up a major 6th to *la* and write the relative minor outside each major, e.g. on the outside of "C" you will write "a".

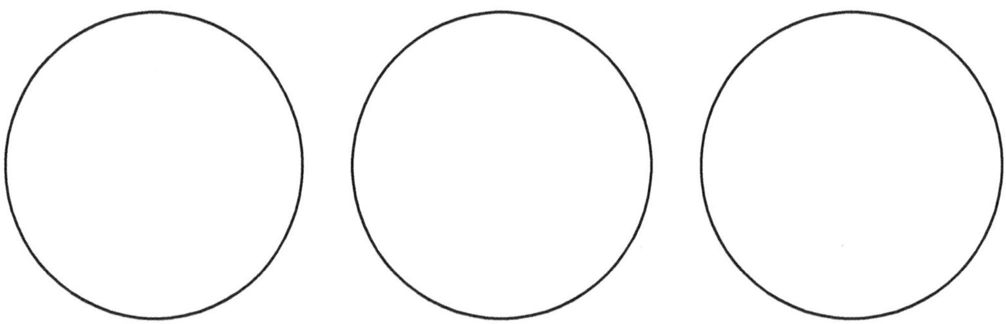

✏ Using the circle of fifths as a reference, write the natural minor scale, ascending and descending, to match each of the key signatures below. Do not add any accidentals for a natural minor scale.

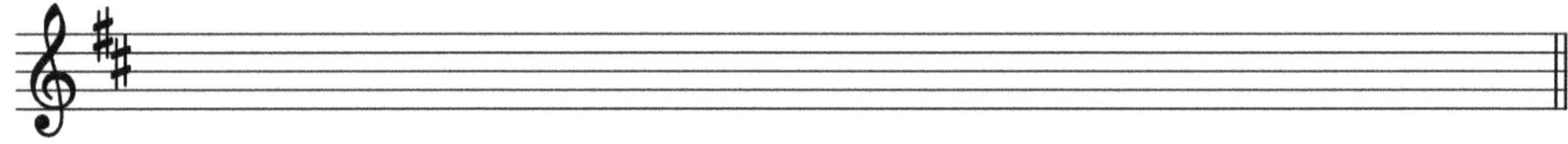

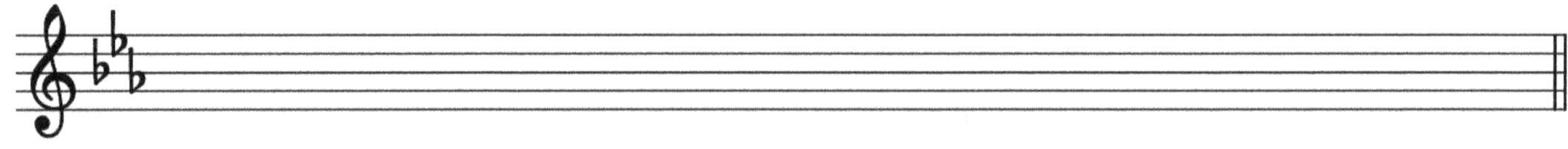

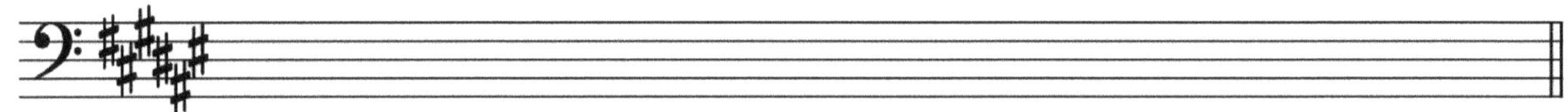

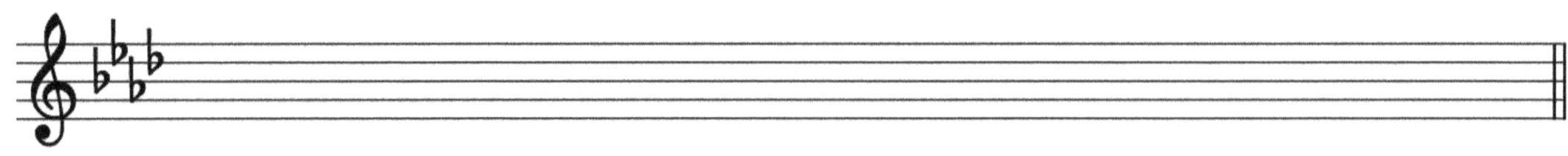

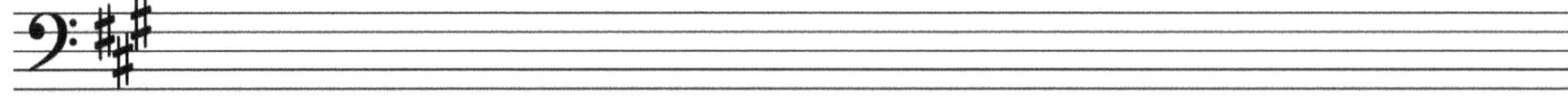

> ➡ The circle of fifths can also be used to work out the order of flats and sharps for writing key signatures. They are always drawn in the same order, no matter how many there are.

🖉 Trace each of the key signatures below, noticing the order of sharps and flats.

🖉 Write the A major scale ascending in half notes. Use a key signature.

🖉 Write the D flat major scale descending in eighth notes. Use a key signature.

🖉 Write the D natural minor scale descending in whole notes. Use a key signature.

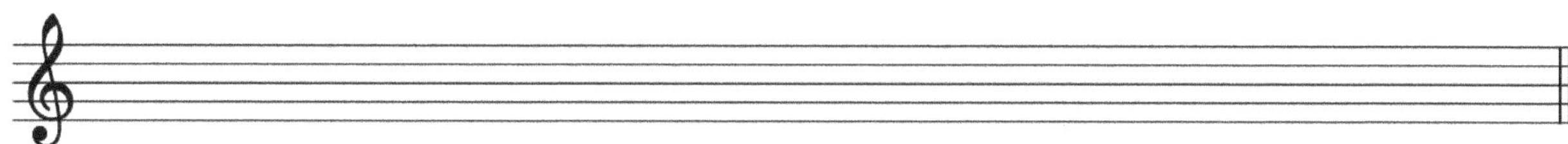

🖉 Write the C sharp natural minor scale ascending in sixteenth notes. Use a key signature.

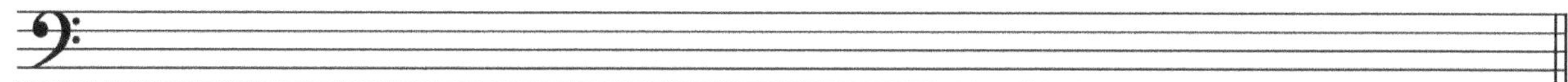

🖉 Write the B flat natural minor scale descending in whole notes. Use a key signature.

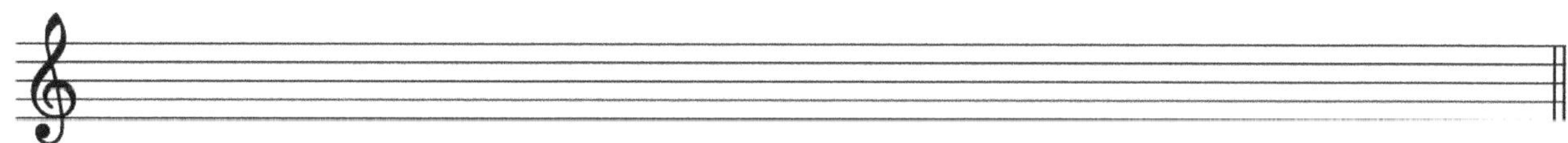

🖉 Write the F natural minor scale ascending in sixteenth notes. Use a key signature.

Add the missing barlines to each melody below.

Add the missing time signatures to each melody below.

Add the missing note values to the rhythm below.

Add the missing rest values to the rhythm below.

➡ Here's an example to help you break down double-dotted notes.

♪.. = ♪ + . + . = ♪..

½   ¼   ⅛   ⅞

New Ingredients: Note values

- • = note/rest value + half of value
- •• = note/rest value + three quarters of value
- ♫ = thirty-second note = ⅛ beat
- ♯ = thirty-second rest = ⅛ beat
- ‖o‖ = breve = 8 beats

 Write one note equal to the total value of each group.

♫ ♪.. = ☐   ♩. ♩.. ♩ = ☐   ♩.. ♩♫ = ☐

♫ ♪.. = ☐   ♪. ♫ ♪ = ☐   ♪.. ♪.. ♪ = ☐

♩ ♪.. = ☐   o. ♪ ♪ ♪ = ☐   ♩.. ♩.. ♩ = ☐

Draw one note value in each box to make the equations correct.

♪ + ☐ + ♪.. = ♩.   ☐ + 𝄽 + 𝄽 = o

𝄽 + ♩ + ☐ = o   𝄽 + ☐ + 𝄾 = ▬

♩ + ♪ + ☐ = ♩.   ♪.. + 𝄾 + 𝄽 = ☐

♫ + ☐ + 𝄾 = ♪..   ♩.. + ♫ + ☐ = o

♩ + ☐ + 𝄾 = ♩.   ♪.. + ☐ + ♩ = ♩.

Sing the given melody 3 times.

Write the solfa initials under the notes and then compose the missing measures. Add suitable dynamics, articulation and tempo mark.

© Copyright 2022 Vibrant Music Limited

Level Up!

Get ready for chapter 3 by answering these questions (without looking back through your book!)

1. Draw a circle of fifths in each box with the major and relative minor.

2. Add the missing note values to the rhythm below.

3. Add the missing barlines to the melody below.

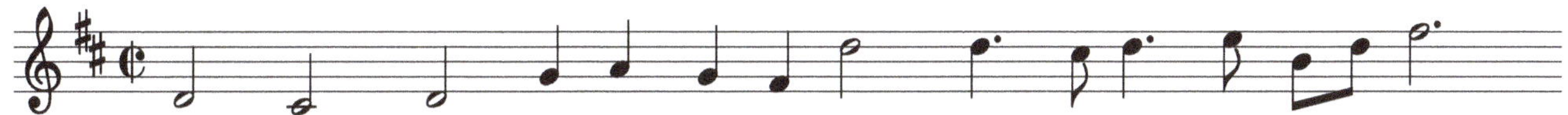

4. Add the missing time signature to the melody below.

5. Compose two measures to complete this melody. Add suitable dynamics, articulation and tempo mark.

6. Write the D flat major scale ascending and descending in quarter notes. Use a key signature.

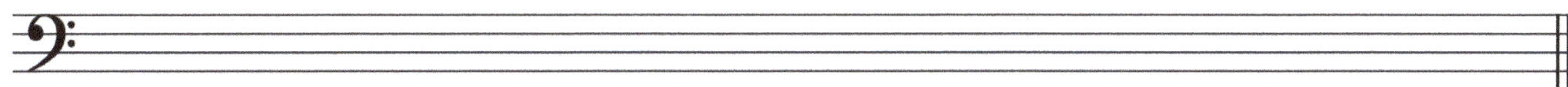

7. Write the C natural minor scale descending in thirty-second notes. Use a key signature.

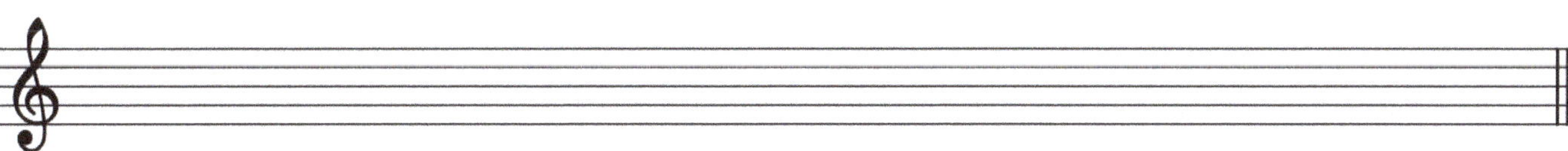

Chapter 3

New Ingredients: Rhythm

$\frac{6}{4}$ = 2 dotted half note beats per measure

$\frac{6}{8}$ = 2 dotted quarter note beats per measure

$\frac{9}{8}$ = 3 dotted quarter note beats per measure

$\frac{12}{8}$ = 4 dotted quarter note beats per measure

➡ These time signatures are compound time signatures.

➡ Compound time signatures have micro and macro beats.

➡ For example, $\frac{8}{8}$ is made up of 8 eighth note micro beats grouped into 2 dotted quarter note macro beats.

🖊 Add the missing barlines to each melody below.

🖊 Add the missing time signatures to each melody below.

> ➡ To make a harmonic scale we raise the seventh note of the natural minor scale by one half step.
>
> ➡ This raised seventh is always shown with an accidental. It does not go in the key signature.

✏️ Write the harmonic minor scale, ascending and descending, to match each of these key signatures.

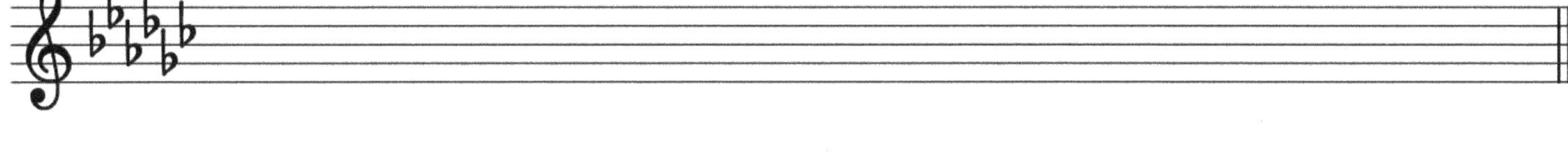

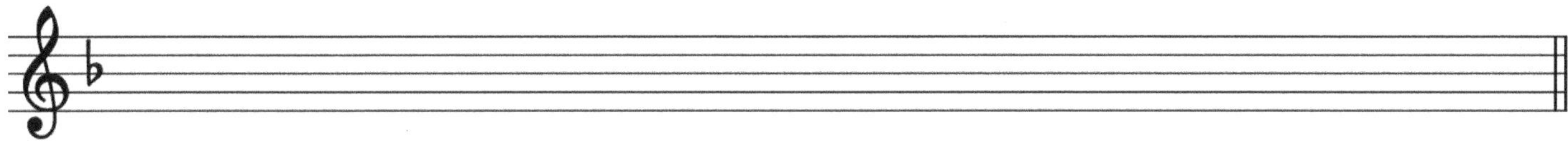

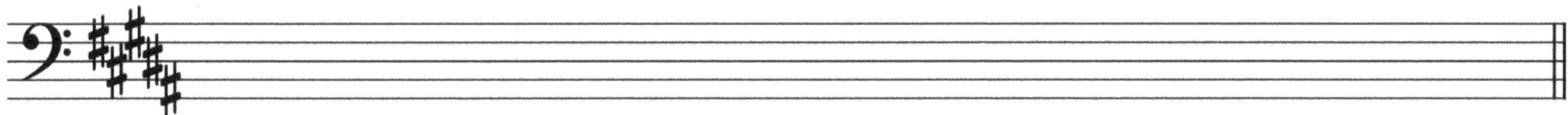

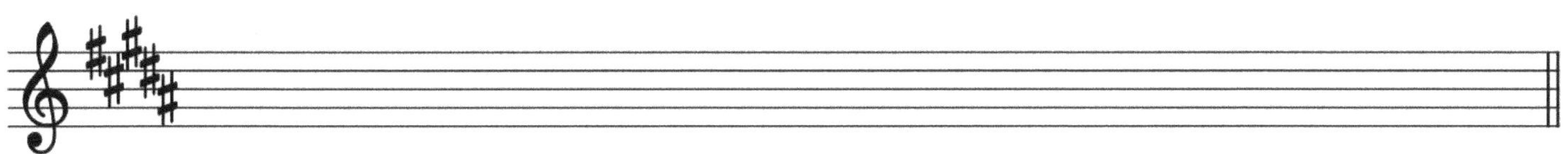

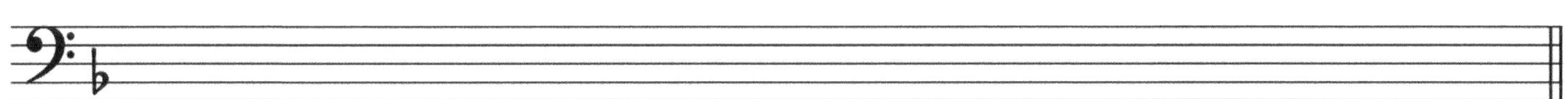

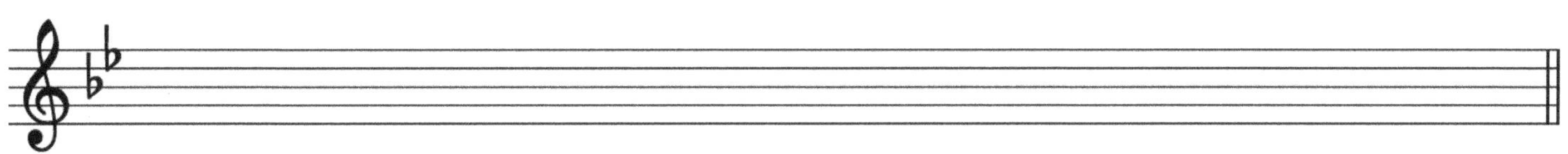

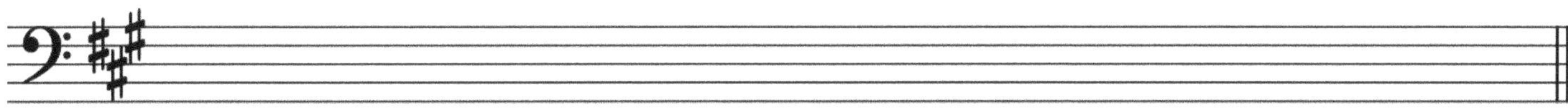

> ➜ The tonic triad is a three note chord with the first note of the scale as the root note.
> ➜ Each key signature has two possible tonic triads, the major and the minor.

🖉 Draw the tonic triad to match each of these major key signatures.

🖉 Draw the tonic triad to match each of these minor key signatures.

🖉 Label each of these chords.

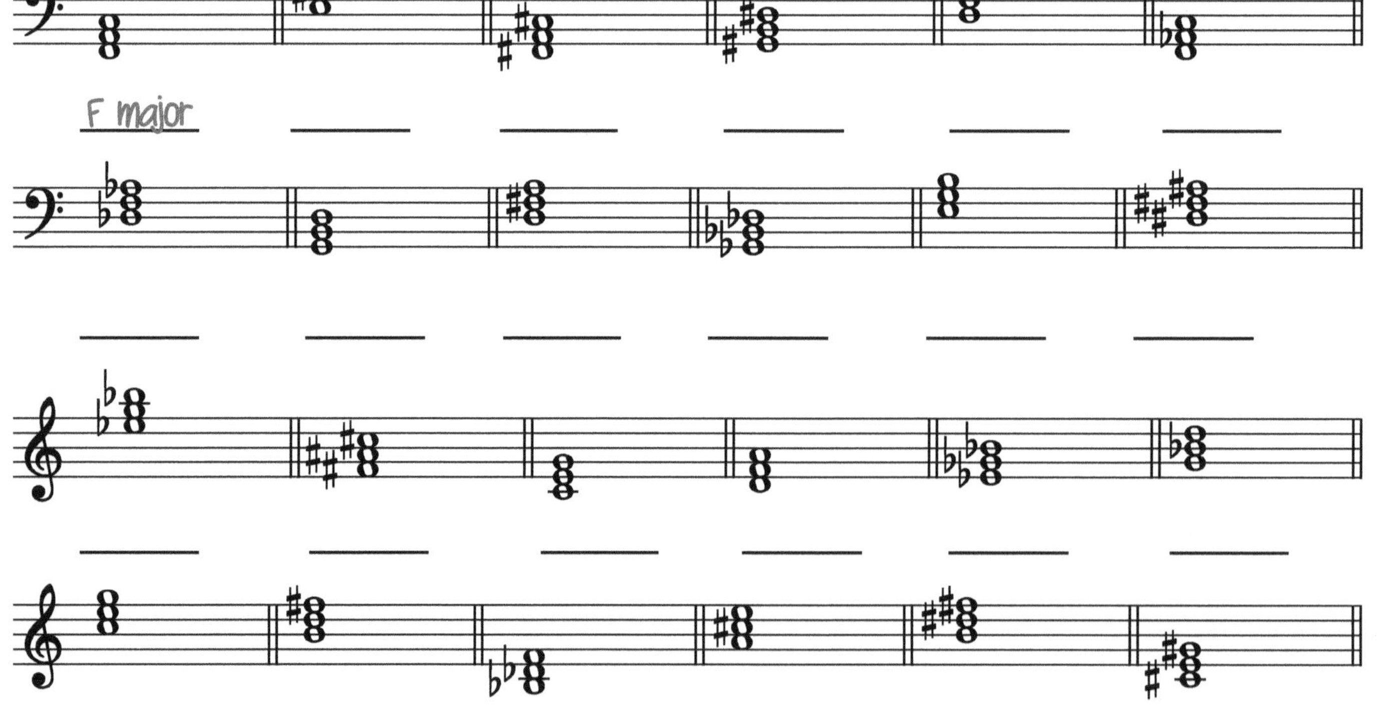

- ➜ Not all intervals in the minor scale are minor intervals.
- ➜ When we describe an interval as major, minor or perfect, we are talking about the number of half steps between the notes.
- ➜ A major interval becomes a minor interval when the top note drops one half step.

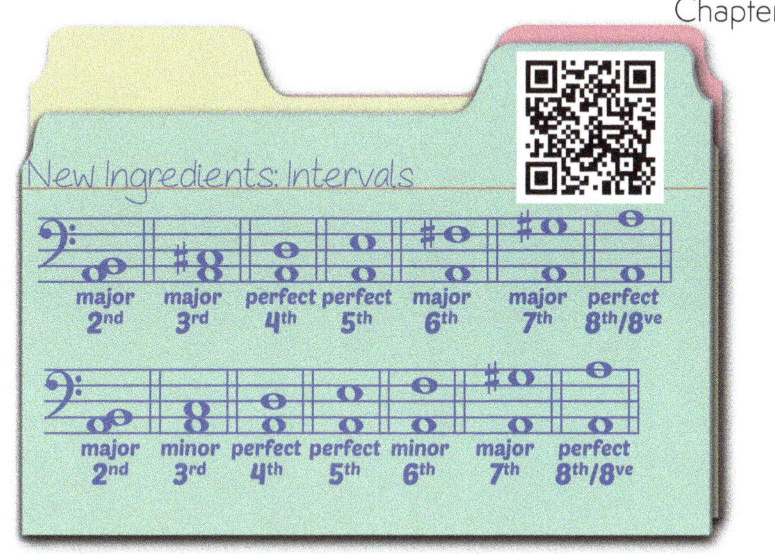

🖊 Label each of these intervals and describe them as minor, major or perfect.

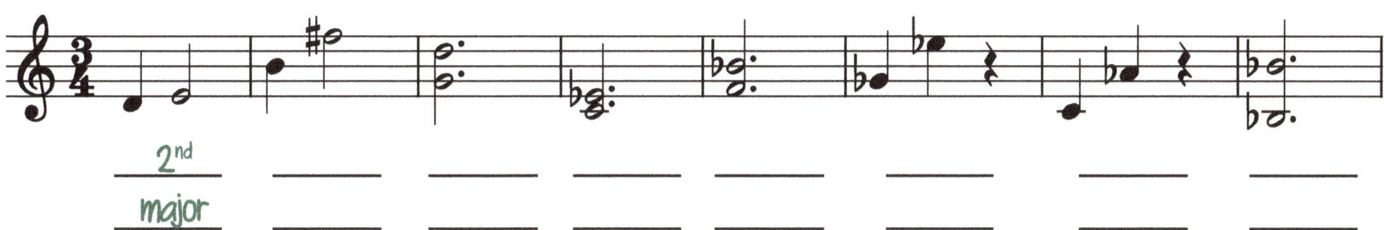

🖊 Add a note above each note to make harmonic intervals. Label the intervals as major, minor or perfect.

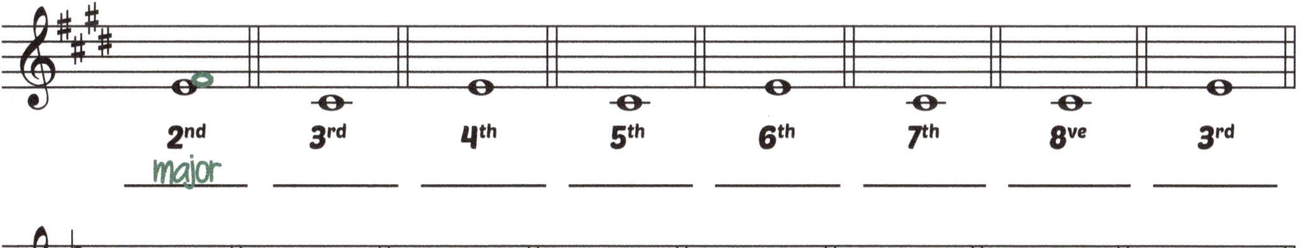

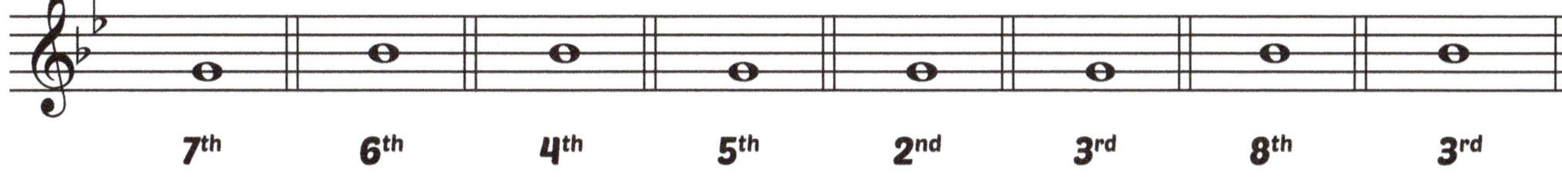

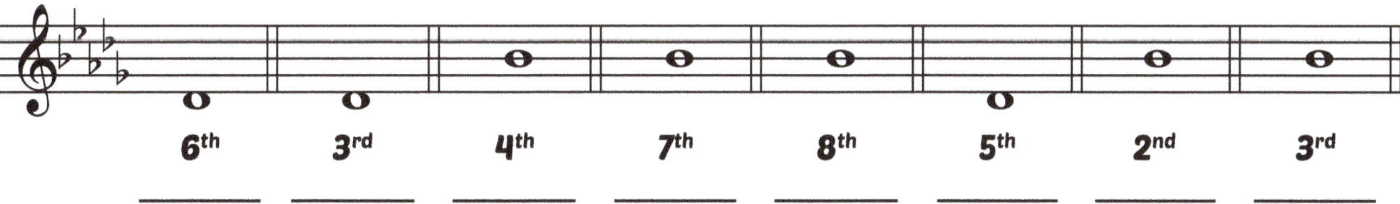

New Ingredients: Musical form

Binary = AB
Ternary = ABA
Rondo = ABACADA
   I = the tonic chord of the major key
   i = the tonic chord of the minor key
   V = the dominant chord of the key

✏️ Complete these questions about the piece above.

1. What is the tempo mark and what does it mean? ________________________________

2. Is the piece in binary, ternary or rondo form? ________________________________

3. Circle every I chord in green and every V chord in red.

4. List the dynamics used in the piece and what they mean. ______________________

____

5. List the articulation marks used in the piece and what they mean. ______________

____

→ Transposing means moving notes to a different spot while keeping the intervals the same.

✎ Transpose these melodies down one octave. Change the clef to make them easier to write.

✎ Transpose these melodies up one octave. Add a clef change to make them easier to write.

✎ Transpose these melodies to the new key signature. Write the solfa names underneath to help you.

Level Up!

Get ready for chapter 4 by answering these questions (without looking back through your book!)

1. What do these symbols and terms mean?

2. Add a new clef and transpose this melody up two octaves. Add the missing time signature.

3. Transpose this melody to the new key signature. Add the missing time signature.

4. Compose two measures to complete this melody. Add suitable dynamics, articulation and tempo mark.

5. Write the F harmonic minor scale ascending in sixteenth notes. Use a key signature.

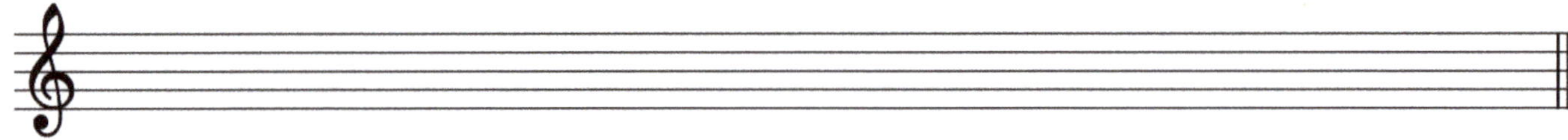

6. Write the E major scale ascending and descending in whole notes. Use accidentals.

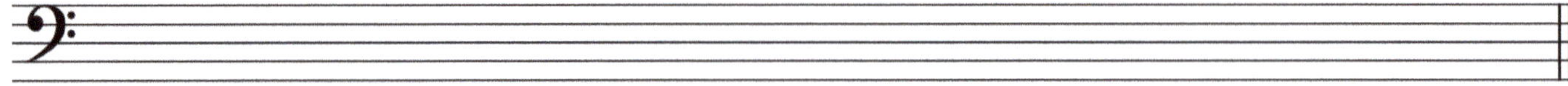

Label each note in solfa and sing the phrase to decide if it is major or minor. Write the scale degrees under the solfa. Transpose each two-measure exercise to the key given on the staff below it.

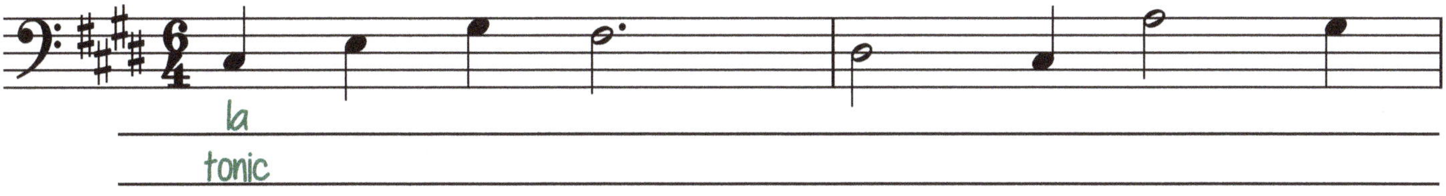

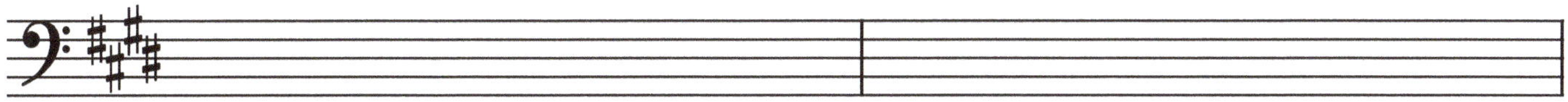

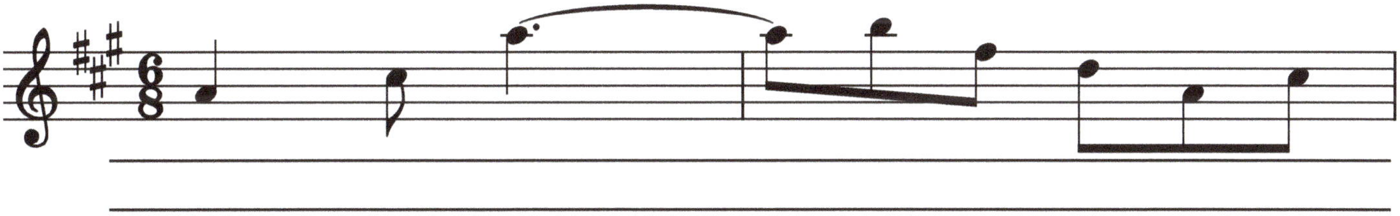

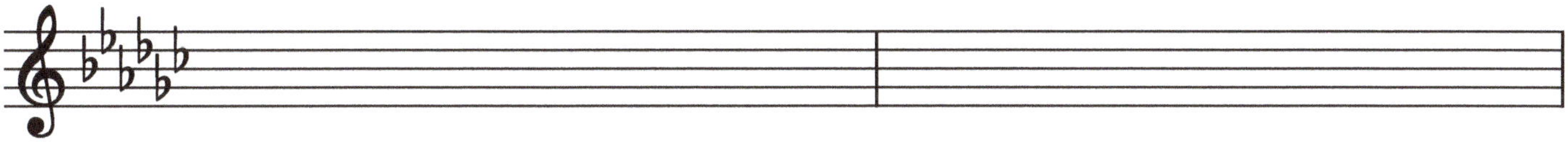

Sing the given measure 3 times in solfa.

Compose 3 more measures to finish the melody. Add appropriate articulation.

Sing the full melody to check your work.

© Copyright 2022 Vibrant Music Limited

🖉 Choose your favorite melody from the opposite page to become your A theme and compose a piece in rondo form. Don't forget the clef, time signature and key signature!

🖉 Add dynamics, articulation and a tempo mark. Give your piece a title and write your name in the composer spot.

> ➜ To make a melodic scale we raise the sixth and seventh note of the natural minor scale by one half step.
>
> ➜ These raised notes are always shown with accidentals.
>
> ➜ The descending melodic minor scale is the same as the natural minor.

🖉 Write the melodic minor scale, ascending and descending, to match each of these key signatures.

🖉 Write the scale degrees under each note and mark the half steps with slurs.

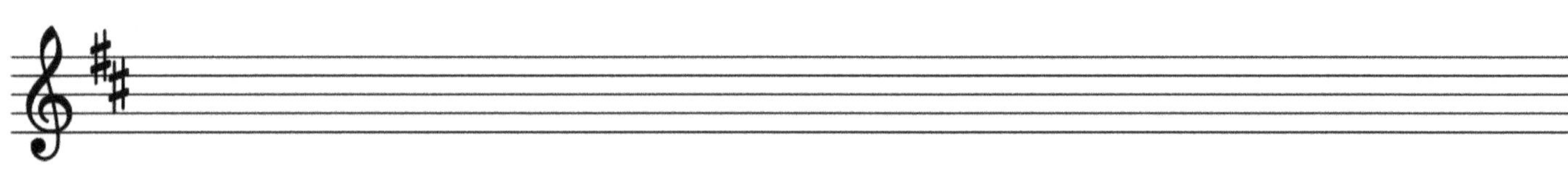

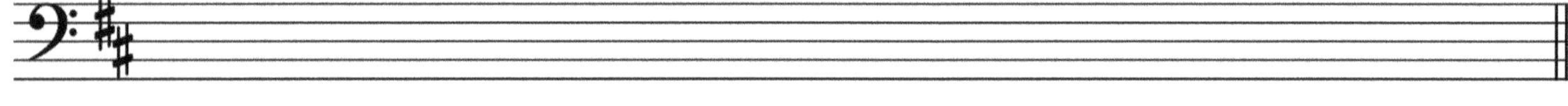

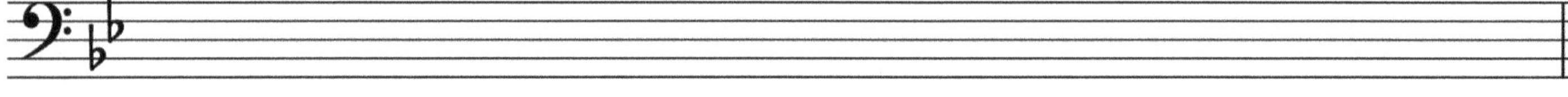

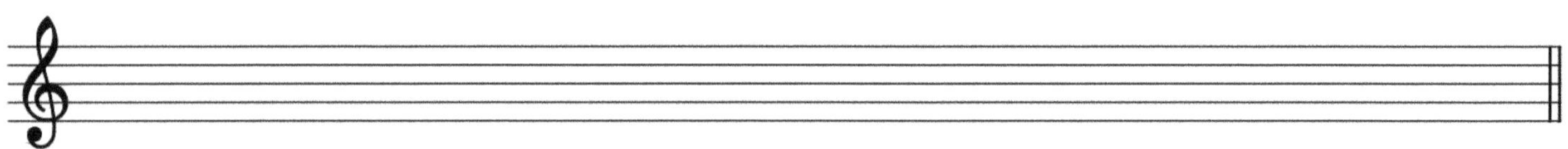

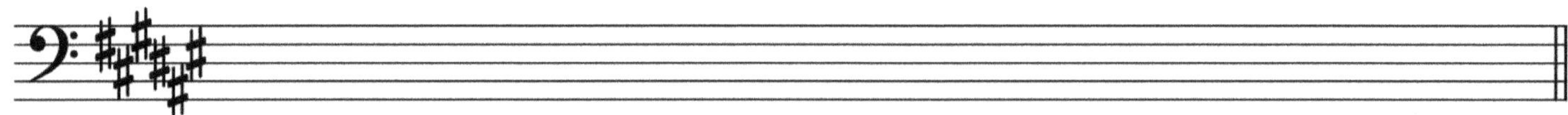

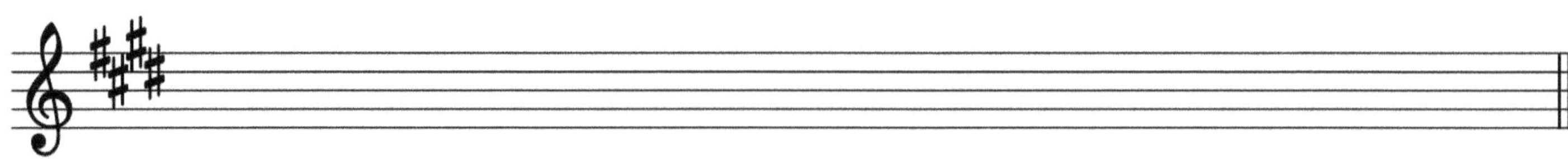

                    © Copyright 2022 Vibrant Music Limited

✏️ Label each of these intervals and describe them as minor, major or perfect.

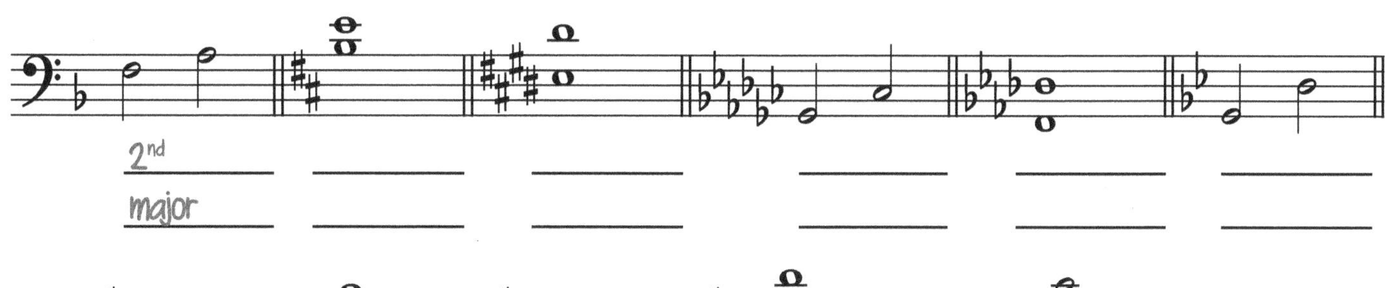

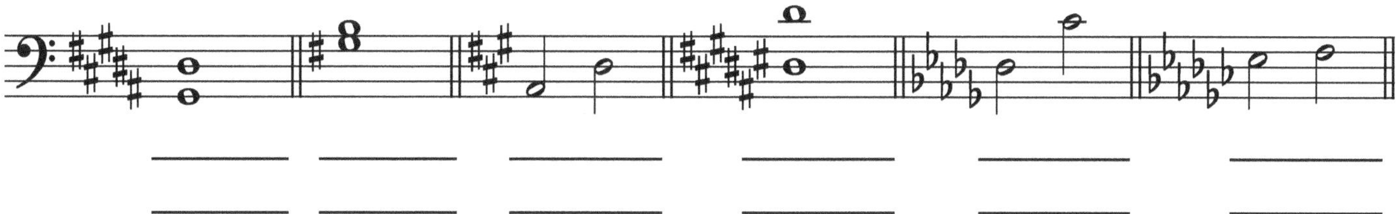

✏️ Add a note after each note to create melodic intervals. Label the intervals as major, minor or perfect.

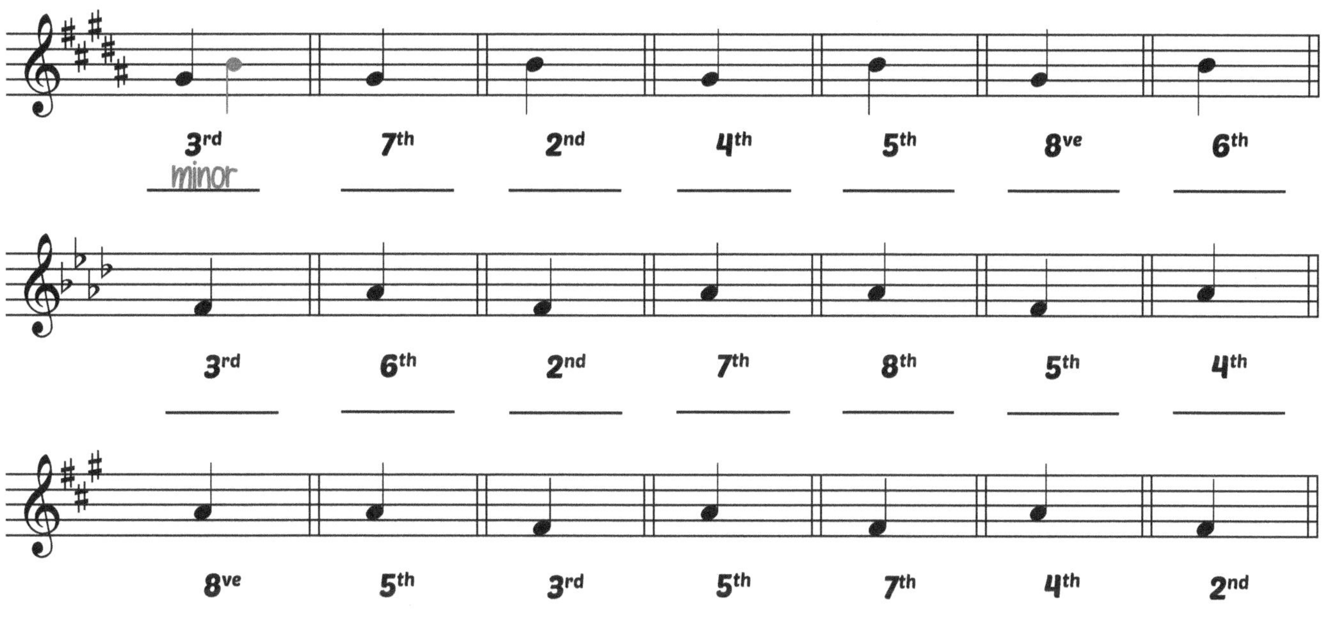

✏️ Write the scale degree under each note from the major scale below.

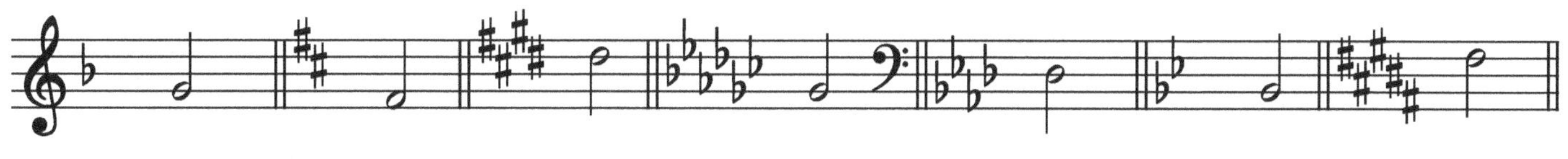

✏️ Write the scale degree under each note from the minor scale below.

✏️ Inside each blue box, add the missing notes to create the chords indicated.

✏️ Add appropriate dynamics, articulation and a tempo mark to each exercise.

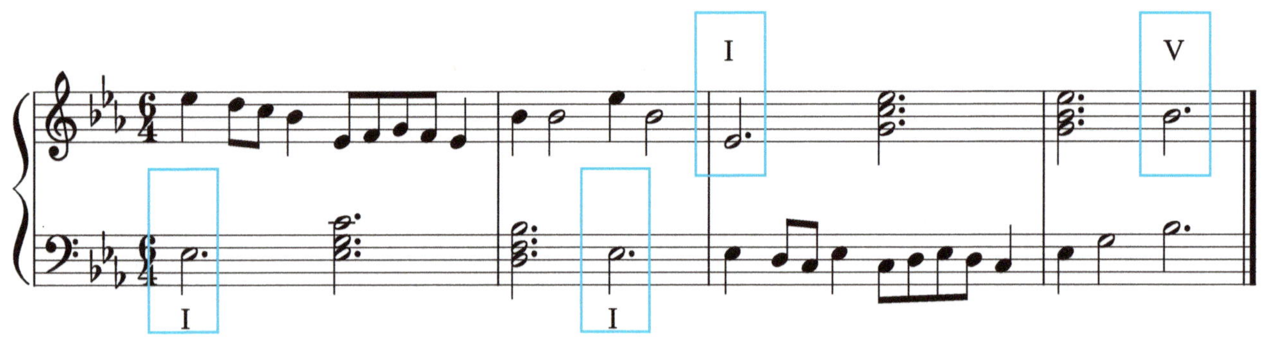

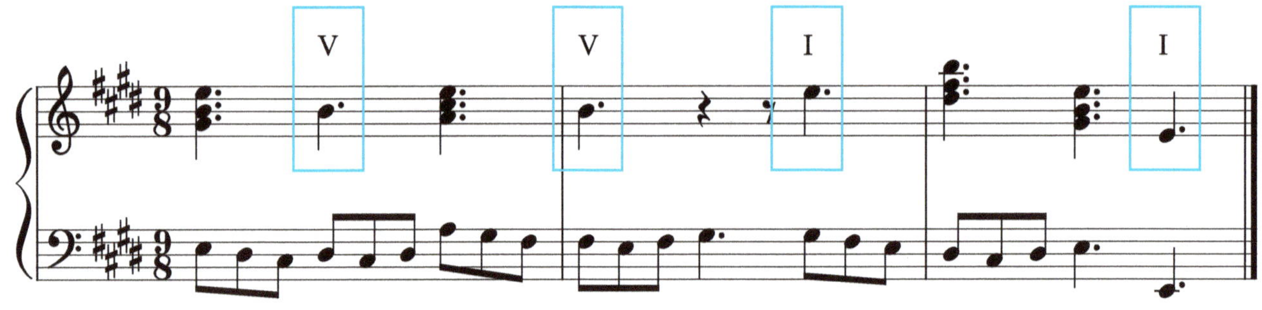

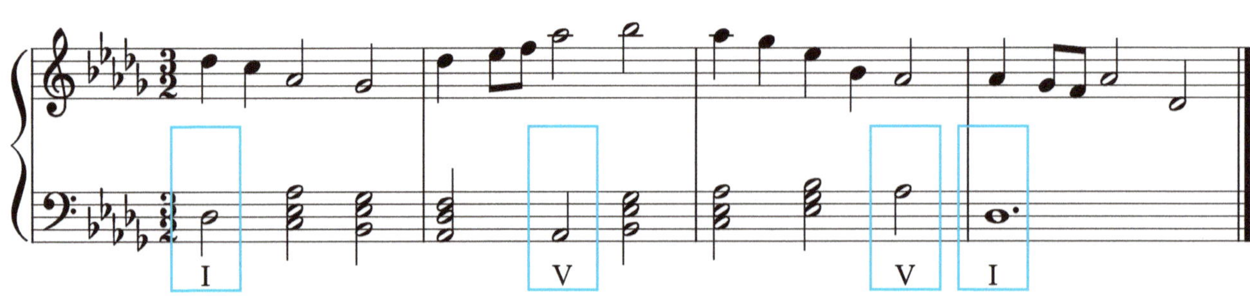

  © Copyright 2022 Vibrant Music Limited

Level Up!

Get ready for chapter 5 by answering these questions (without looking back through your book!)

1. What do these symbols and terms mean?

dolce = ___________________________   *sf* = ___________________________

grazioso = ___________________________   **enharmonic** = ___________________________

allegretto = ___________________________   ♮ = ___________________________

poco rall. = ___________________________   **half step** = ___________________________

con moto = ___________________________   ♪♪♪ (3) = ___________________________

2. Write the equivalent scale degree for each solfa note from the major scale.

re = __________________   *so* = __________________   *mi* = __________________

fa = __________________   *la* = __________________   *ti* = __________________

3. Add a note after each note to create melodic intervals. Label the intervals as major, minor or perfect.

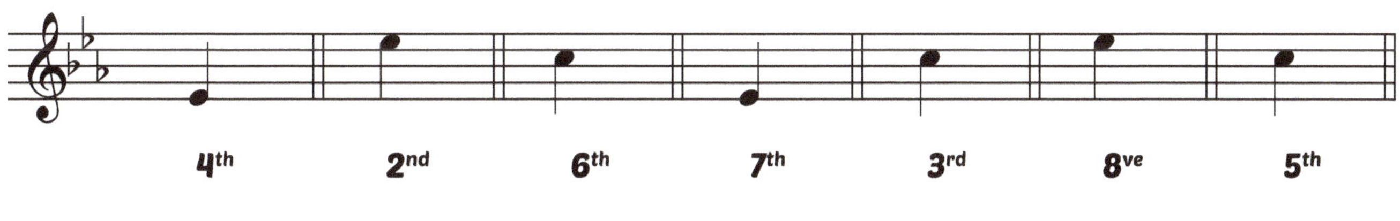

4th   **2nd**   **6th**   **7th**   **3rd**   **8ve**   **5th**

_____   _____   _____   _____   _____   _____   _____

4. Write the D sharp melodic minor scale ascending in half notes. Do not use a key signature.

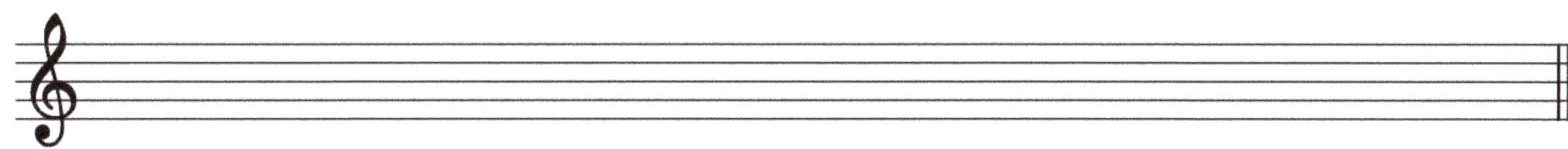

5. Write the A flat major scale descending in eighth notes. Use a key signature.

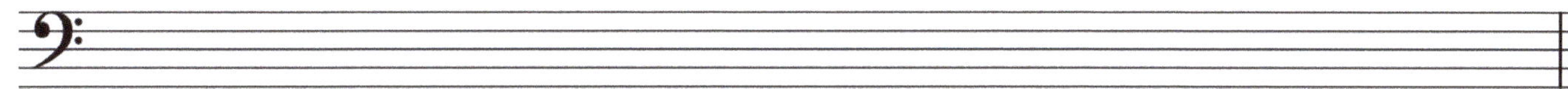

6. Add the missing rest or rests at each arrow below.

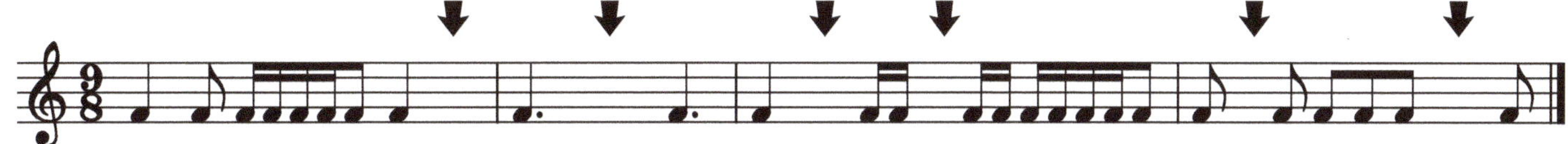

- Eighth notes, sixteenth notes and thirty-second notes are beamed or joined together in groups to make reading easier.
- In simple time signatures, beamed notes are grouped into quarter note beats.
- In compound time signatures, beamed notes are grouped into the macro beats, e.g. in $\frac{6}{4}$ they would be grouped in dotted half note beats and in $\frac{9}{8}$ they would be grouped in dotted quarter note beats.
- A whole measure of eighth notes only can be beamed in $\frac{3}{8}$, $\frac{3}{4}$ and $\frac{2}{4}$. In other time signatures like $\frac{4}{4}$ and $\frac{3}{2}$, eighth notes can be beamed in groups of 4.
- Rests are grouped in a similar way to beamed notes, to show the beats clearly.
- A whole measure rest is shown with a whole rest, no matter what the time signature is.

✎ Rewrite this rhythm with the notes correctly grouped.

✎ Fill in the missing rest or rests at each arrow.

✎ Draw one rest value in each box to make the equations correct.

✎ Rewrite this melody on the staff below with the notes and rests correctly grouped.

✎ Write one note equal to the total value of each group.

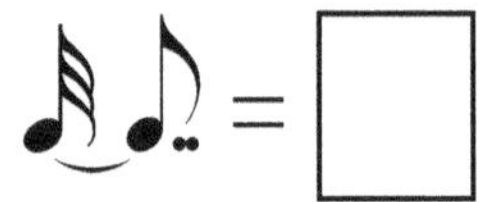

✏️ Write one note equal to the total value of each group.

✏️ Rewrite this melody on the staff below with the notes correctly grouped.

✏️ Draw one note value in each box to make the equations correct.

✏️ Rewrite this melody on the staff below with the notes and rests correctly grouped.

✏️ Draw one rest value in each box to make the equations correct.

✏️ Rewrite this melody on the staff below with the notes and rests correctly grouped.

✏️ Draw one rest value in each box to make the equations correct.

✎ Write the melodic minor scale to match this key signature.

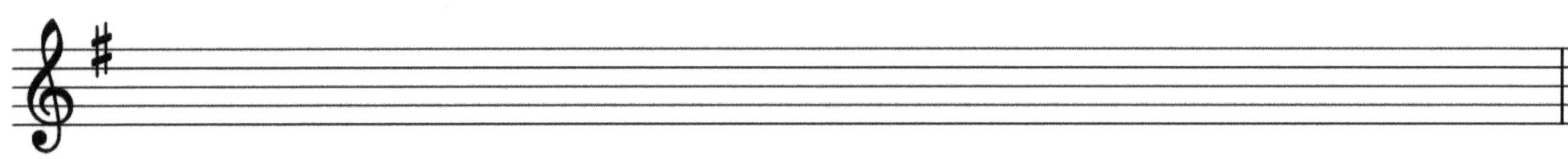

✎ Write the E flat major scale. Do not use a key signature.

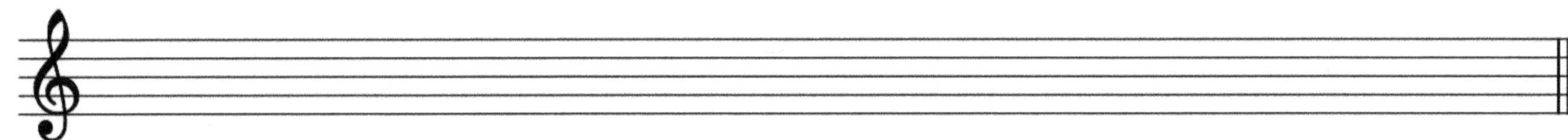

✎ Write the scale degree under each note from the major scale below.

✎ Write the natural minor scale to match this key signature.

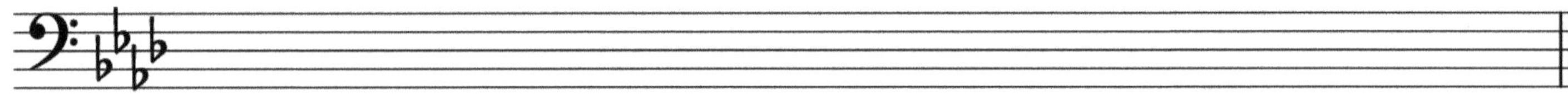

✎ Write the B flat harmonic minor scale. Do not use a key signature.

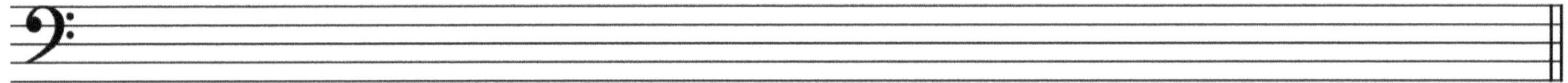

✎ Write the tonic chord to match each of these minor key signatures.

✎ Write the harmonic minor scale to match this key signature.

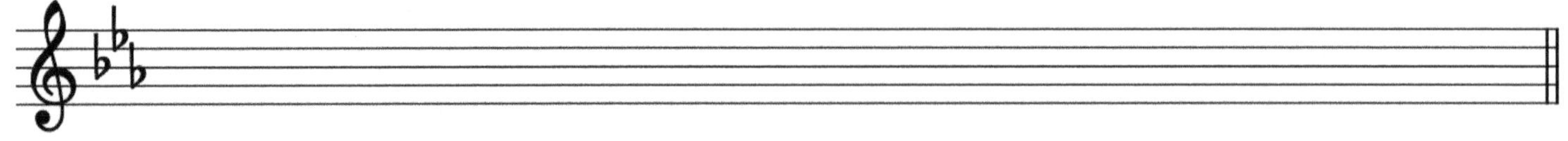

🖊 Write the E melodic minor scale. Do not use a key signature.

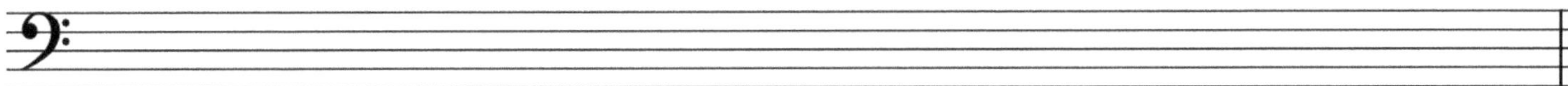

🖊 Add an accidental to one note in each measure to make the interval labels correct.

🖊 Write the major scale to match this key signature.

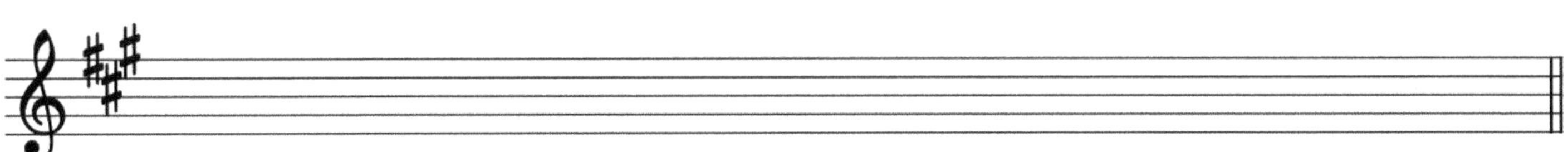

🖊 Write the harmonic minor scale to match this key signature.

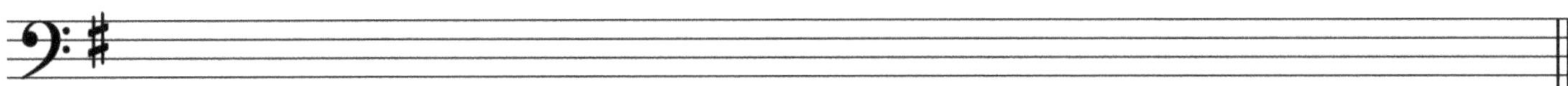

🖊 Write the major scale to match this key signature.

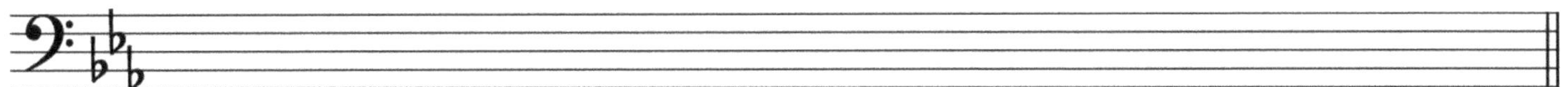

🖊 Write the scale degree under each note from the minor scale below.

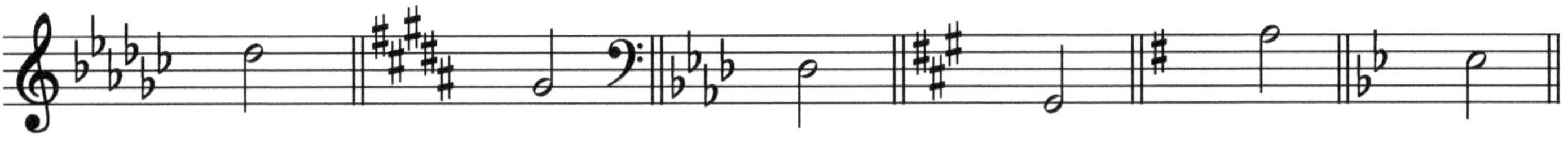

🖊 Write the F sharp major scale. Do not use a key signature.

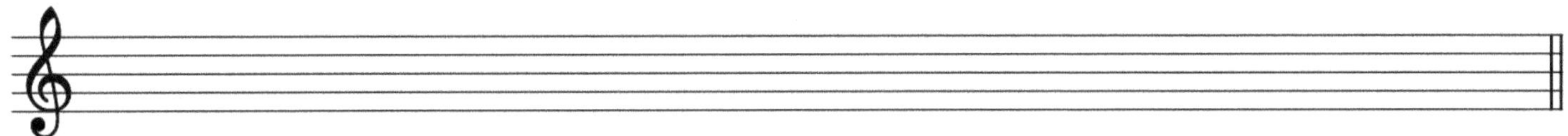

🎤 Sing the given measure 3 times in solfa.

✏️ Compose 3 more measures to finish the melody. Add appropriate articulation.

🎤 Sing the full melody to check your work.

                    © Copyright 2022 Vibrant Music Limited

Choose one melody from the opposite page to become your A theme and compose a piece in binary form. Don't forget the clef, time signature and key signature!

Add dynamics, articulation and a tempo mark. Add a title and your name as the composer.

Choose one melody from the opposite page to become your A theme and compose a piece in ternary form. Don't forget the clef, time signature and key signature!

Add dynamics, articulation and a tempo mark. Add a title and your name as the composer.

Level Up!

Get ready for chapter 6 by answering these questions (without looking back through your book!)

1. Label each note in solfa and sing the phrase to decide if it is major or minor. Write the scale degrees under the solfa. Transpose this melody to the key given on the staff below it.

2. Fill in the missing rest or rests at each arrow.

3. Write the melodic minor scale to match this key signature. Mark the half steps with slurs.

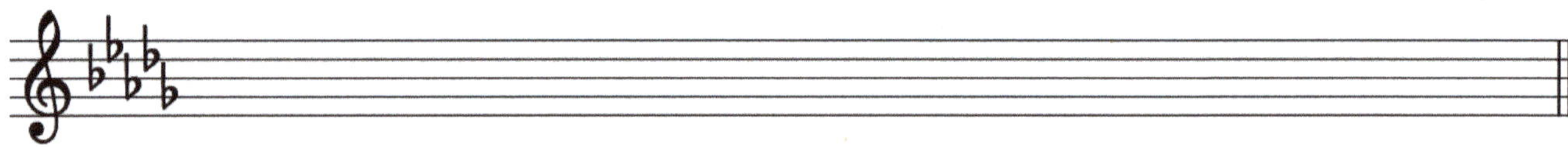

4. Rewrite this melody on the staff below with the notes correctly grouped.

5. Add a second note in each measure to make these harmonic intervals.

Level Up!
The final test! Answer these questions without looking back through your book!

1. Write the equivalent scale degree for each solfa note from the minor scale.

do = _____________________		*ti* = _____________________		*mi* = _____________________

la = _____________________		*re* = _____________________		*fa* = _____________________

2. Write the harmonic minor scale, ascending in whole notes, to match this key signature.

3. Transpose this melody down one octave.

4. Compose 3 more measures to finish the melody. Add appropriate articulation and dynamics.

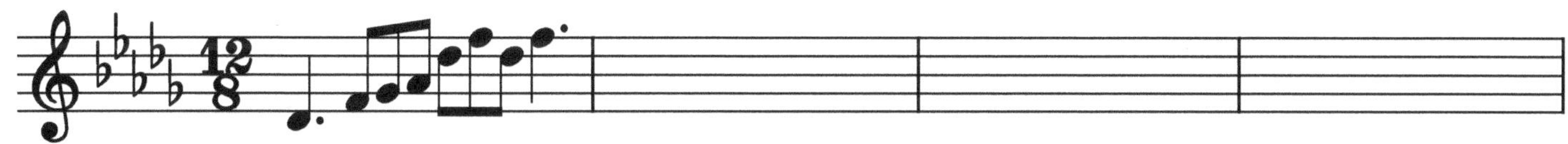

5. Rewrite this melody on the staff below with the notes and rests correctly grouped.

6. Draw one note value in each box to make the equations correct.

7. Add an accidental to one note in each measure to make the interval labels correct.

8. Write the major scale, descending in thirty-second notes, to match this key signature. Mark the half steps with slurs.

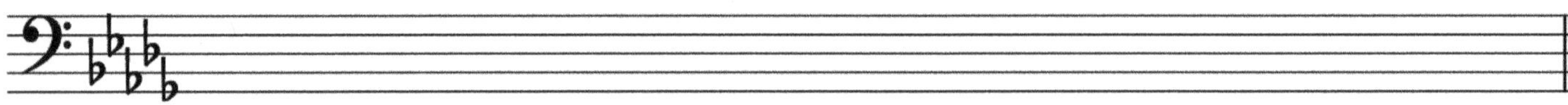

9. Transpose this melody into the new key.

10. Write the melodic scale, ascending and descending, to match this key signature. Write the scale degree and solfa name under each note.

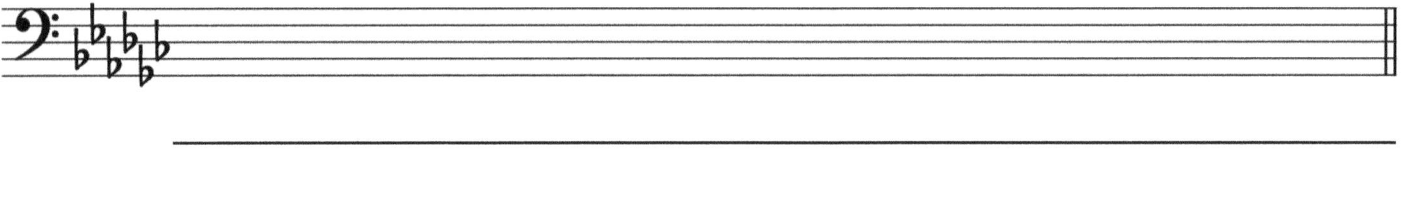

11. What do these symbols and terms mean?

Binary form = ______________________   ⸙ = ______________________

Ternary form = ______________________   = ______________________

Rondo form = ______________________   ♮ = ______________________

espressivo = ______________________   = ______________________

giocoso = ______________________   = ______________________

Answer the following questions about the piece above.

12. What is the key of this piece? _______________________________

13. What is the relative key? ___________________________

14. Is the time signature simple or compound? _______________________________

15. Is the piece in duple, triple or quadruple time? _______________________________

16. Circle a submediant and put a square around a supertonic.

17. Is the piece in binary, ternary or rondo form? _______________________________

18. What is the name of the shortest note value? _______________________________

19. The piece should start loudly, get gradually softer from measure 6 and be very soft in the last measure.
    Add dynamic markings to show this.

20. The piece should be played quite slowly. Add a tempo mark to show this.

21. The player should pause and hold the last note for longer than its value. Add a symbol to show this.

Term Review Cheat Sheet

♬	sixteenth note	$\frac{1}{4}$ beat
♪	eighth note	$\frac{1}{2}$ beat
♪.	dotted eighth note	$\frac{3}{4}$ beat
♫	eighth note triplet	$\frac{1}{3}$ beat each
♩	quarter note	1 beat
♩.	dotted quarter note	$1\frac{1}{2}$ beats
♩	half note	2 beats
♩.	dotted half note	3 beats
o	whole note	4 beats
⅞	sixteenth rest	$\frac{1}{4}$ beat
⁊	eighth rest	$\frac{1}{2}$ beat
𝄽	quarter rest	1 beat
—	half rest	2 beat
—	whole rest	whole measure
$\frac{2}{4}$	simple duple time	2 quarter note beats in a measure
$\frac{3}{4}$	simple triple time	3 quarter note beats in a measure
$\frac{4}{4}$	simple quadruple time	4 quarter note beats in a measure
C	common time	4 quarter note beats in a measure
₵	cut time	2 half note beats in a measure
$\frac{2}{2}$	simple duple time	2 half note beats in a measure
$\frac{3}{2}$	simple triple time	3 half note beats in a measure
$\frac{4}{2}$	simple quadruple time	4 half note beats in a measure
$\frac{3}{8}$	simple triple time	3 eighth note beats in a measure
enharmonic		same sound written differently
half step		notes directly beside each other
whole step		two half steps
♯	sharp	one half step higher
♭	flat	one half step lower
♮	natural	not sharp or flat
pp	pianissimo	very soft
p	piano	soft
sempre p	sempre piano	always soft
mp	mezzo piano	moderately soft
mf	mezzo forte	moderately loud
f	forte	loud
sempre f	sempre forte	always loud
ff	fortissimo	very loud
sf		emphasised
fp		loud then immediately soft
<	crescendo	getting louder
>	diminuendo	getting softer
cresc.	crescendo	getting louder
dim.	diminuendo	getting softer

decresc.	decrescendo	getting softer
rall.	rallentando	getting slower
rit.	ritenuto	getting slower
ritard.	ritardando	getting slower
poco rall.	poco rallentando	getting a little slower
poco rit.	poco ritenuto	getting a little slower
accelerando		gradually getting faster
a tempo		back to original speed
con moto		with movement
meno mosso		less movement
più mosso		more movement
♩	staccato	sharply detached
♩	accent	with emphasis
♩	tenuto	with a fuller whole step
♩	marcato	with strong emphasis
♩♩♩	portato/semi-staccato	slightly detached
𝄐	fermata	pause
⌒	slur	play smoothly
𝄆 𝄇	repeat marks	repeat this section
8va		one octave higher than written
8vb		one octave lower than written
	1st time measure/1st ending	
	2nd time measure/2nd ending	
𝄢.		depress sustain pedal
✻		release sustain pedal
presto		fast
vivace		lively
allegro		quick & lively
allegretto		moderately quick
moderato		moderate speed
alla marcia		like a march
andante		walking pace
larghetto		fairly slowly
largo		slowly
adagio		slowly
lento		slowly
dolce		sweetly
grazioso		gracefully
cantabile		with a singing tone
giocoso		playful/merry
maestoso		majestic
espressivo		expressive

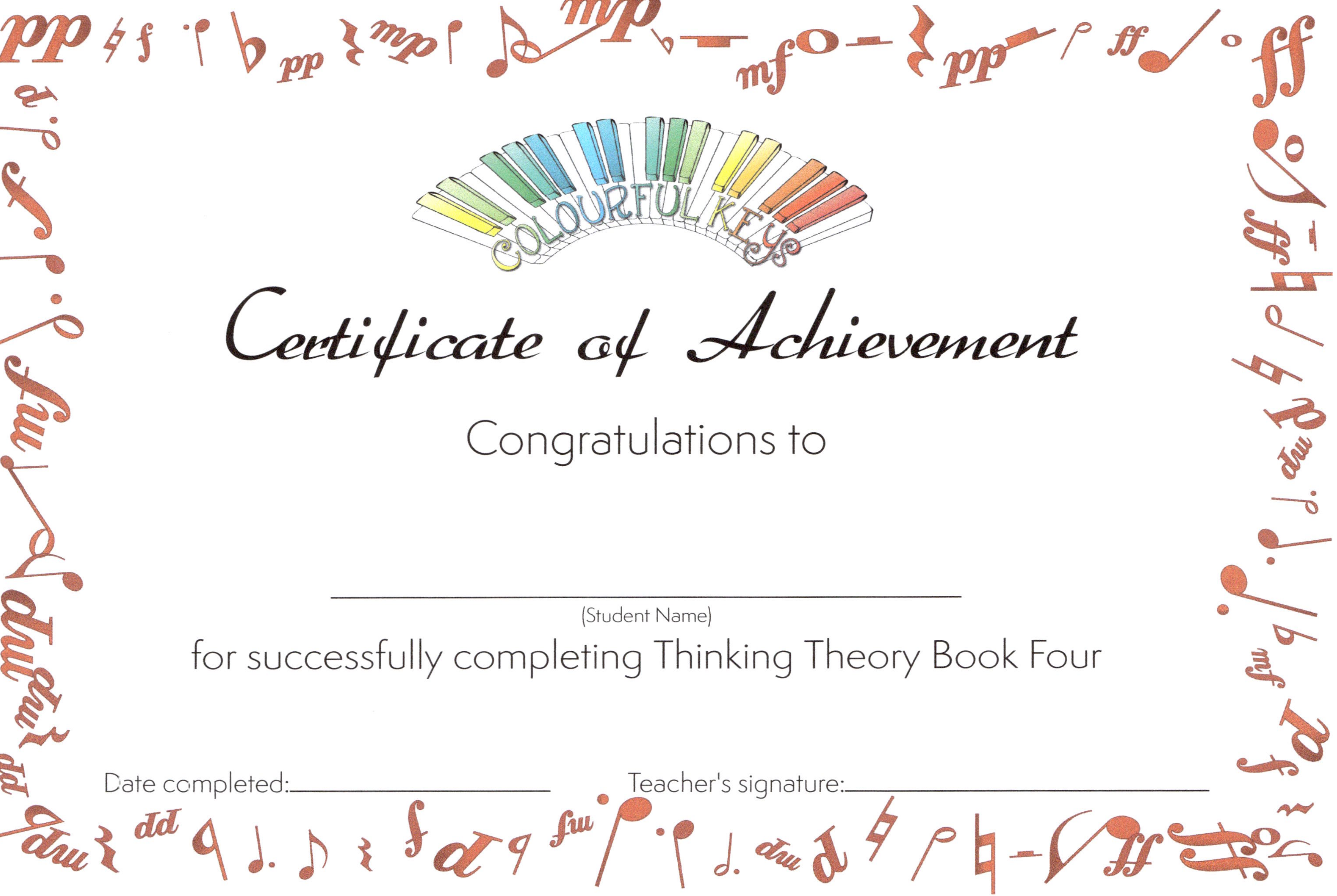

Certificate of Achievement

Congratulations to

____
(Student Name)

for successfully completing Thinking Theory Book Four

Date completed:_______________   Teacher's signature:_______________